LITTLE SPOTTED CAT

by Alyssa Satin Capucilli

illustrations by Dan Andreasen

Dial Books for Young Readers
New York

For Judith Satin, my very own Mama Cat,
with love! —A.S.C.

For Katrina —D.A.

Published by Dial Books for Young Readers

A division of Penguin Young Readers Group

345 Hudson Street

New York, New York 10014

Text copyright © 2005 by Alyssa Satin Capucilli

Illustrations copyright © 2005 by Dan Andreasen

Designed by Lily Malcom

Text set in Italia Bold

Manufactured in China on acid-free paper

1 3 5 7 9 10 8 6 4 2

Library of Congress Cataloging-in-Publication Data

Capucilli, Alyssa.

Little Spotted Cat / by Alyssa Satin Capucilli ; illustrations by Dan Andreasen.

p. cm.

Summary: Little Spotted Cat gets into all sorts of mischief
when he decides to play rather than take his nap.

ISBN 0-8037-2692-9

[1. Cats—Fiction. 2. Naps (Sleep)—Fiction. 3. Behavior—Fiction.]

I. Andreasen, Dan, ill. II. Title.

PZ7.C179 Li 2005

[E]—dc21

2002008360

The art was prepared using oil on gessoed illustration board.

Mama Cat called,
"It's time for your nap, you Little Spotted Cat."

"No, no! Meow!" said Little Spotted Cat.
"Now it's time for play!"
Little Spotted Cat jumped up, up, up.
The flowerpot fell down, down, CRASH!

"Oh no! Meow!"
said Little Spotted Cat.
"What will Mama Cat say?"

And Mama Cat called,
"It's time for your nap,
you Little Spotted Cat."

"No, no! Meow!"
said Little Spotted Cat.
"Now it's time for fun!"

Little Spotted Cat push-pushed the yarn.
He pull-pull-pulled the yarn.
In and out! Here and there!
Yarn, yarn, yarn, EVERYWHERE!

"Oh no! Meow!" said Little Spotted Cat.
"What will Mama Cat say?"

And Mama Cat called,
"It's time for your nap,
you Little Spotted Cat."

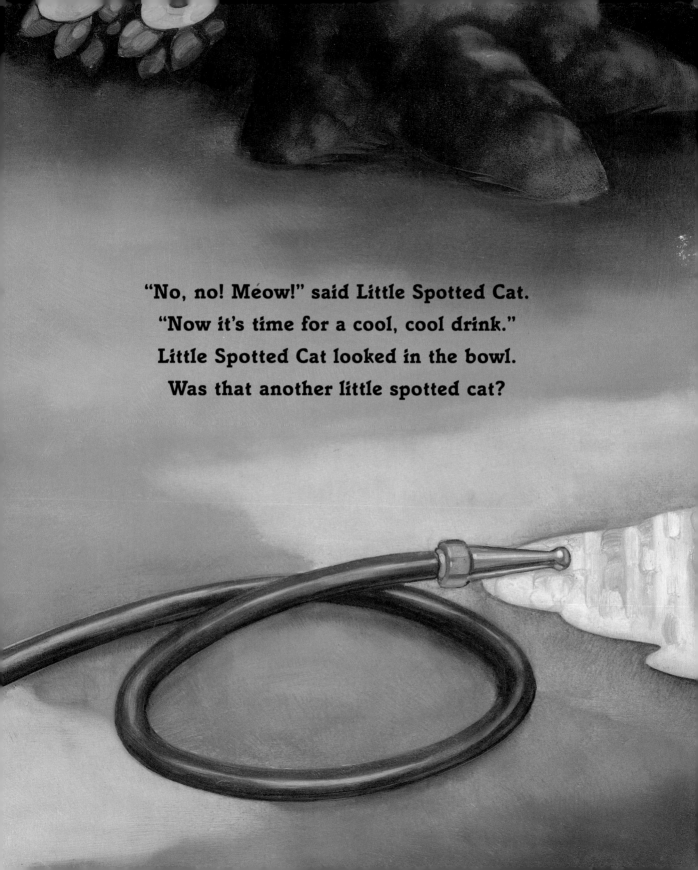

"No, no! Meow!" said Little Spotted Cat.
"Now it's time for a cool, cool drink."
Little Spotted Cat looked in the bowl.
Was that another little spotted cat?

Slip-slap-SPLASH!

"Oh no! Meow!" said Little Spotted Cat.
"What will Mama Cat say?"

And Mama Cat called, loud-louder this time,
"Where are you, you Little Spotted Cat?
You must take your nap!"

"No, no! Meow!" said Little Spotted Cat.
"Now it's time for some sun-sunny fun!"
A grasshopper came hop-hopping by.
"Hello! Meow!" said Little Spotted Cat.
"I will hop-hop-hop with you!"

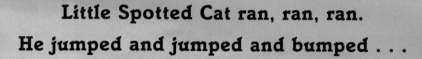

Little Spotted Cat ran, ran, ran.
He jumped and jumped and bumped . . .

KER-PLOP!

"Oh no! Meow!" said Little Spotted Cat.
"Here comes Mama Cat now!"

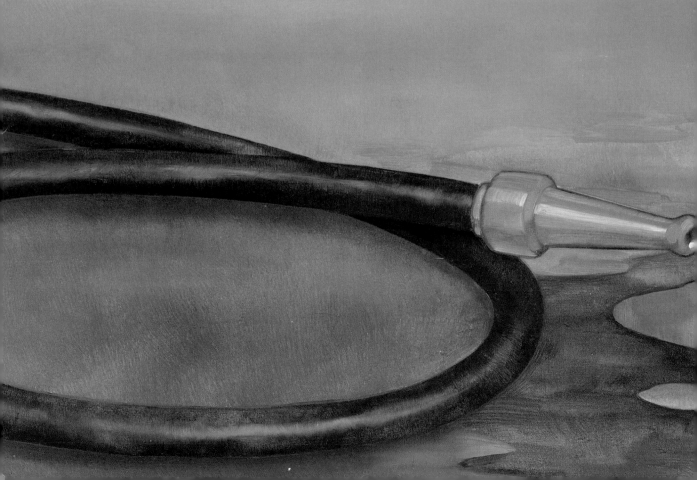

And Mama Cat said,
"Here you are, my wet, muddy
Little Spotted Cat.

"You must wash your paws,
you must refill the bowl,
roll up the yarn,
and pick up the flowerpot.

"And now, my Little Spotted Cat,
you are all clean and cozy and . . .

you *must* take your nap!"

But Little Spotted Cat just went,
"Purr-purr-purr" and . . .
"Snore-snore-snore."

He was already fast asleep
and dreaming
little spotted
cat-nap dreams.